YIKES!

what's **eating** you?

written by **mike janulewicz**

"for Jan, probably the best boy in the world"

designed by mike jolley

edited by dugald steer

Simon & Schuster Books for Young Readers
An imprint of Simon & Schuster Children's Publishing Division
1230 Avenue of the Americas, New York, New York 10020

Copyright © 1997 by The Templar Company plc
Pippbrook Mill, London Road, Dorking, Surrey RH4 1JE, Great Britain.
Photographs copyright © 1997 by Science Photo Library and individual copyright holders and
copyright © FPG/Robert Harding Picture Library

Printed in Hong Kong

First Edition
10 9 8 7 6 5 4 3 2 1

ISBN 0-689-81520-4
Library of Congress Catalog Card Number 96-71979

YIKES!

Your body, up *close!*

You may know yourself pretty well. You probably look at your hair, eyes, nose, and skin every day. Not many surprises, are there? But what about up close? What do you really look like? When you get very close you'll find all sorts of things on you, and in you that look pretty weird. In fact, those things might make you feel just a little queasy. Especially when you remember you've got them with you twenty four hours a day!

take a

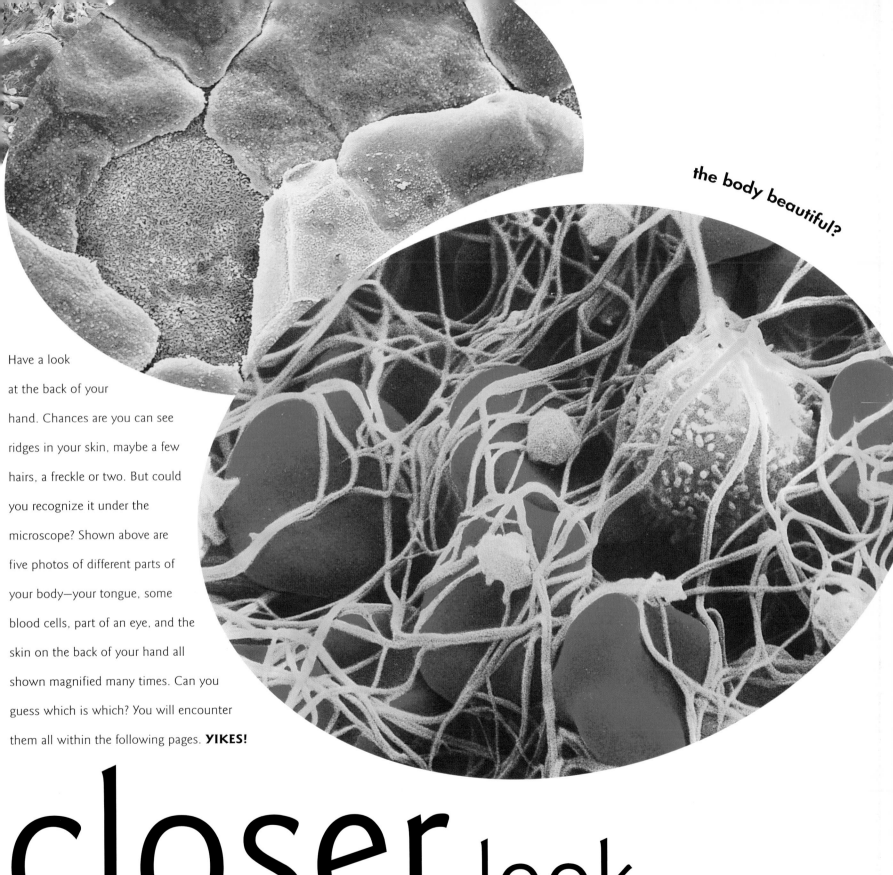

Have a look at the back of your hand. Chances are you can see ridges in your skin, maybe a few hairs, a freckle or two. But could you recognize it under the microscope? Shown above are five photos of different parts of your body—your tongue, some blood cells, part of an eye, and the skin on the back of your hand all shown magnified many times. Can you guess which is which? You will encounter them all within the following pages. **YIKES!**

closer look . . .

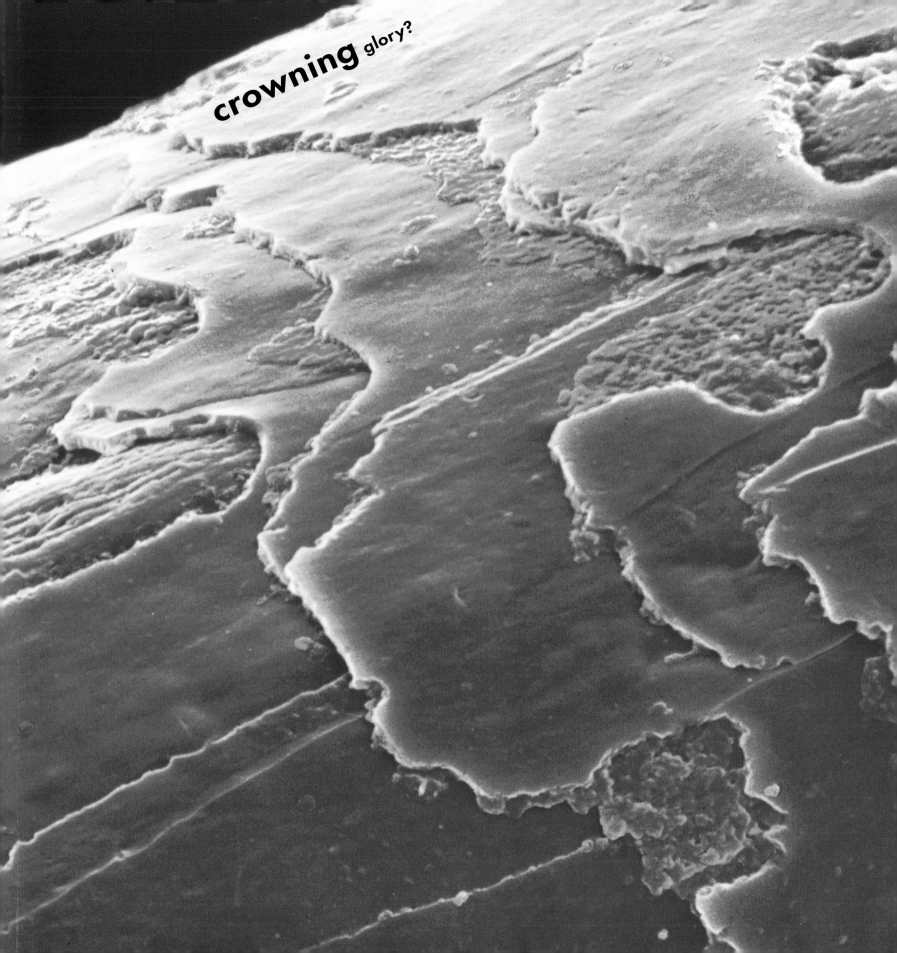

crowning glory?

..... a brush with danger?

If you think this is tree bark you are barking up the wrong tree. But you may have had a close shave with the pink worms. There could be as many as 200,000 of them on your head at this very moment! Do they give you goose bumps? You won't find a single one on the palms of your hands or the soles of your feet. Take a look under the flap if you're ready to face the bald facts.

say ahhhh...

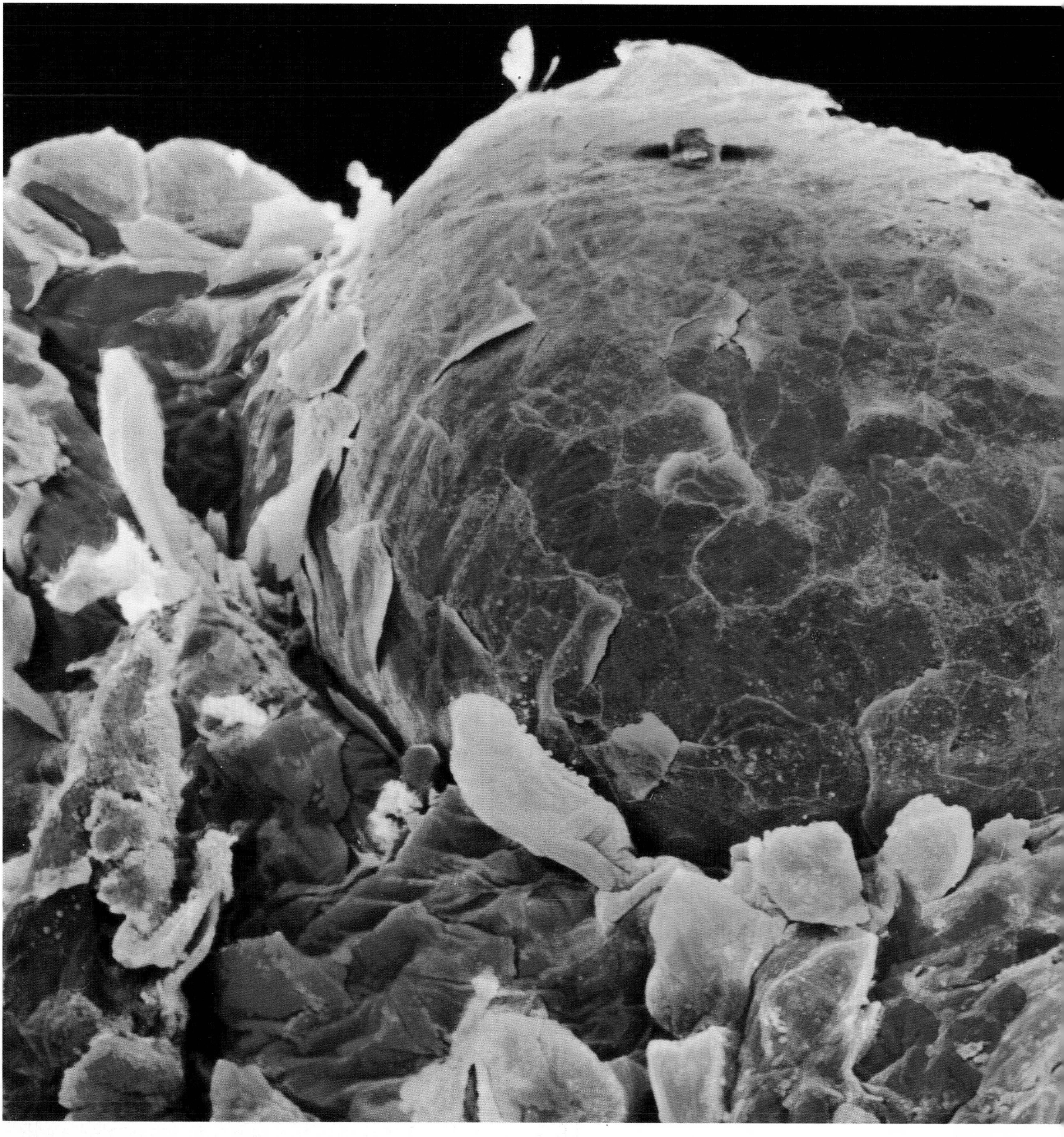

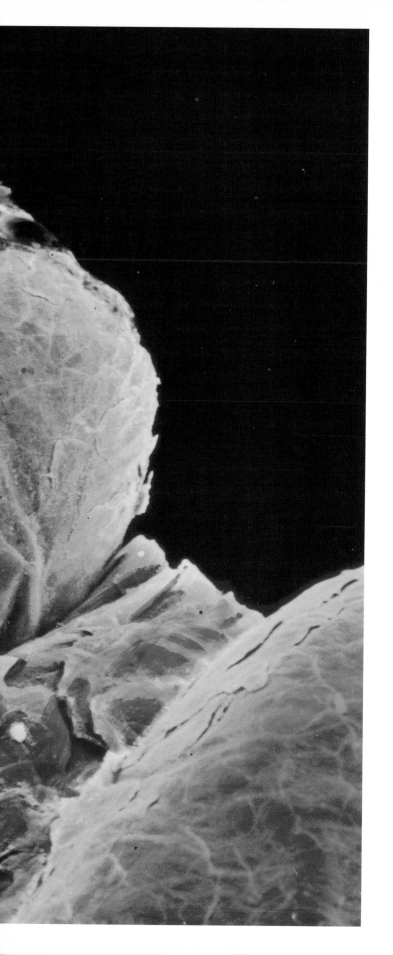

what is it?

Believe it or not, this blob is part of the strongest muscle in your body. You don't use it to lift weights, but without it you couldn't talk very well. It's wet and slippery and helped you out with your lunch. It even told you what flavor topping was on that pizza last night. Was that chicken finger-lickin' good? Or was that burger just gross? We'd love to give you another clue, but our lips are sealed.

the answer is...

brush up!

...putting the bite on

You may think this crater is on some alien planet, but it's a lot nearer than you imagine. Don't expect us to fill you in if you don't know where it is. You should know the drill by now. If you've forgotten to do a certain something after every meal, then this could be what is happening to you. Chew on this one for a while before you turn the page.

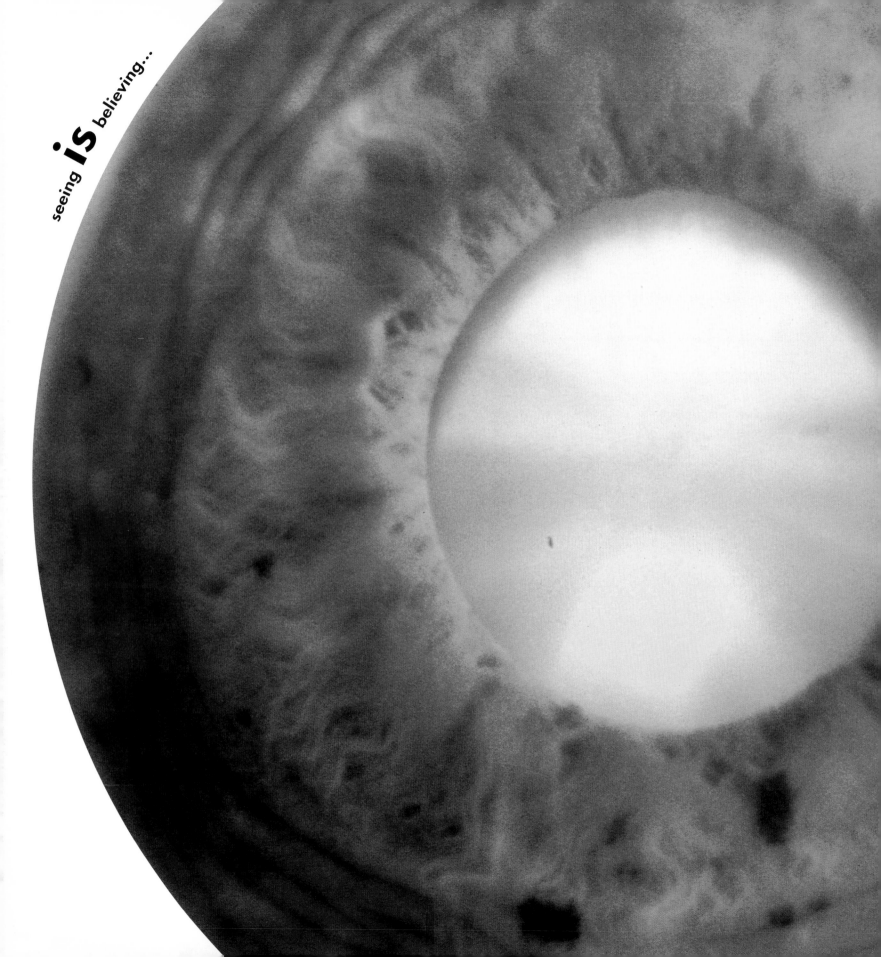

seeing **is** believing...

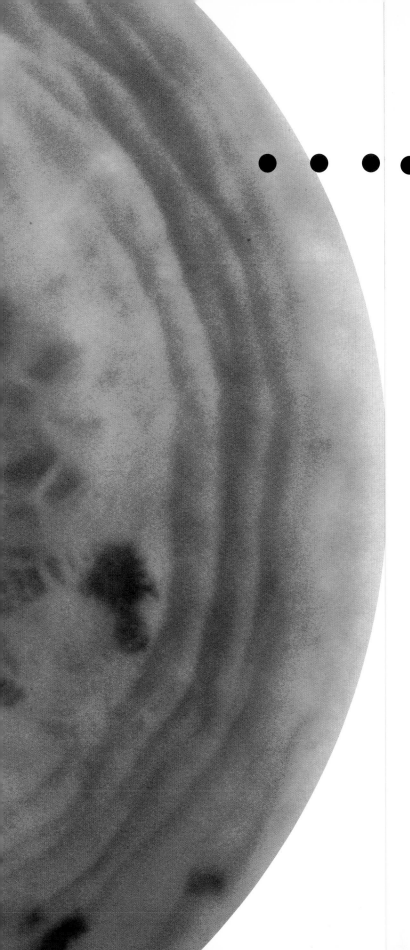

. . . . what a sight!

Can't you see what this is? Take a closer look. Still can't see? Well, it's one of a pair and although this one's brown, it could be blue, gray, or even green. Each one moves about a hundred thousand times a day and without them you'd definitely be in the dark. If you are in the dark now, then you'd better lift up that flap right away and take a quick peek.

a slice of cake, **anyone?**

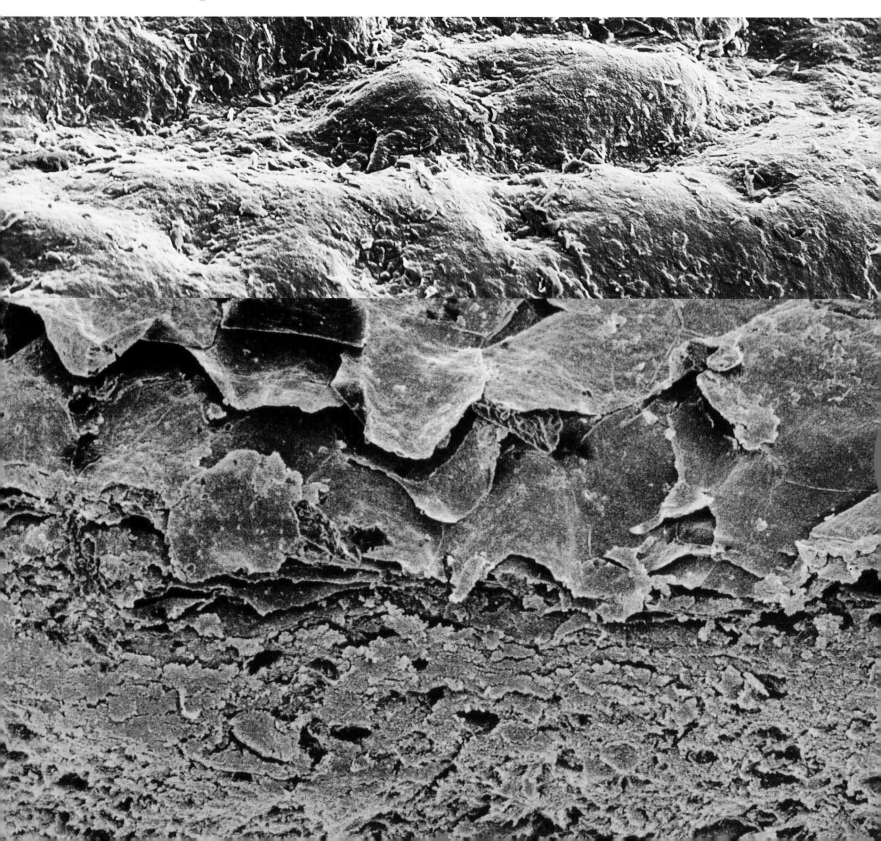

yummy!

it's a **beauty...**

This fellow won't eat you alive—he only likes the dead parts. And there are dead bits falling off you all the time. He's horrible enough to make you jump out of your skin, but he hides and waits for it to drop off—bit by bit!

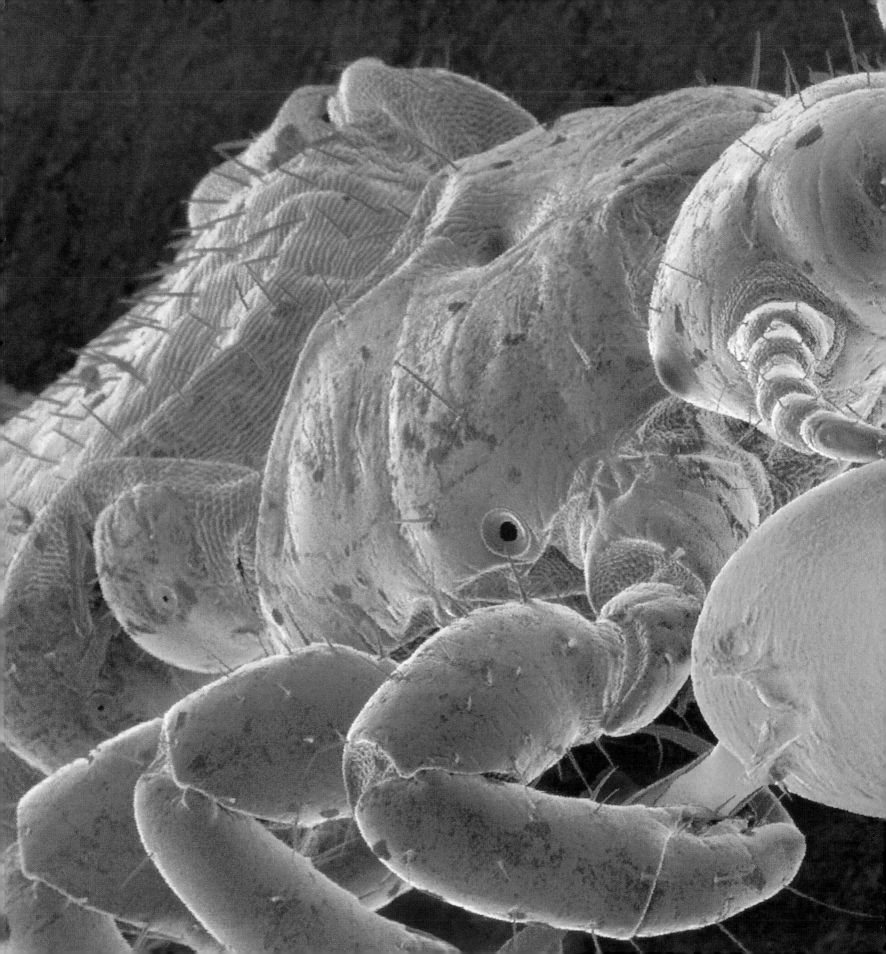

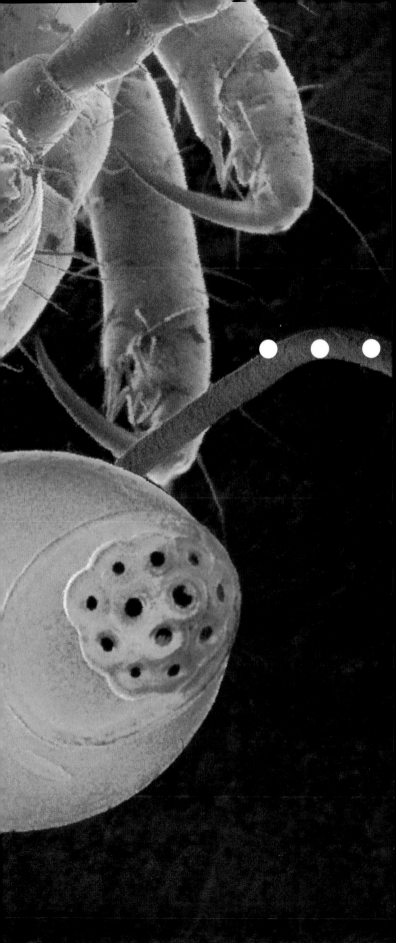

.... **guess**
who?

So

who's your friend with the

Easter egg? How many is she bringing

for lunch? We think she's a creep. But you

could be the perfect host. We could make a lot of

lousy jokes but we know you're too clever for that!

Still can't remember her name? There's no use in

scratching your head about it. If you're

itching to know, it's . . .

Time: 08.00 hours

Place: bathroom

motive: getting ready for school

evidence: fingerprints, hair, skin, toothbrush

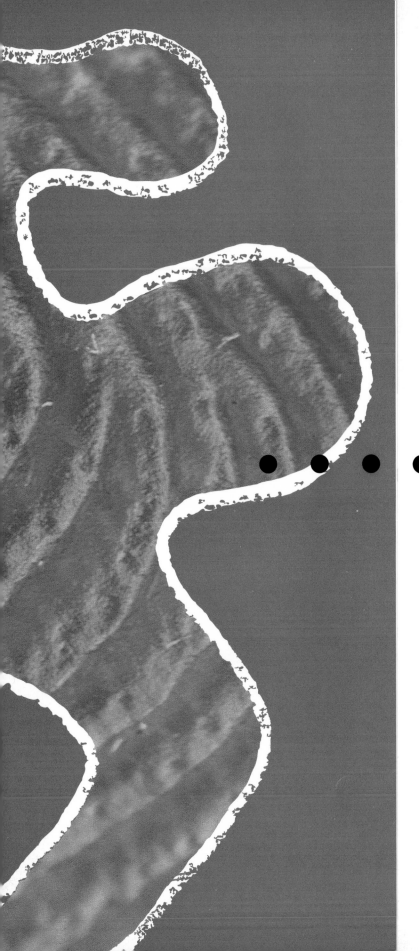

.....body

of evidence

suspect: ....?

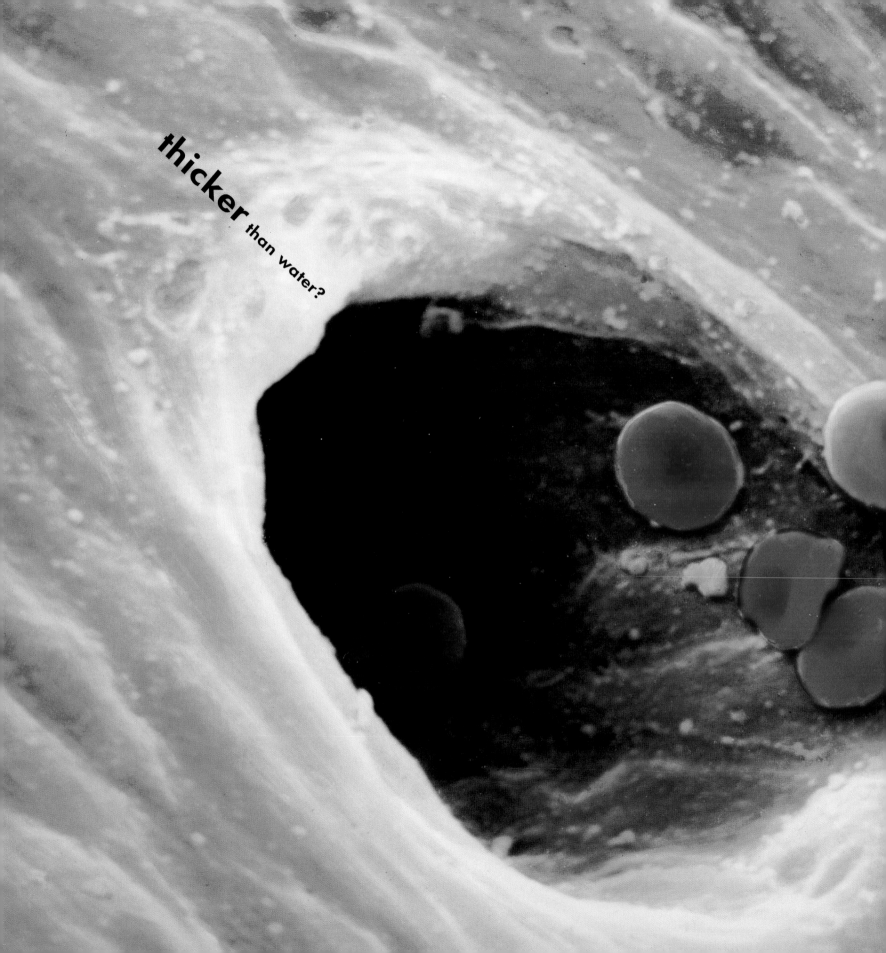

thicker than water?

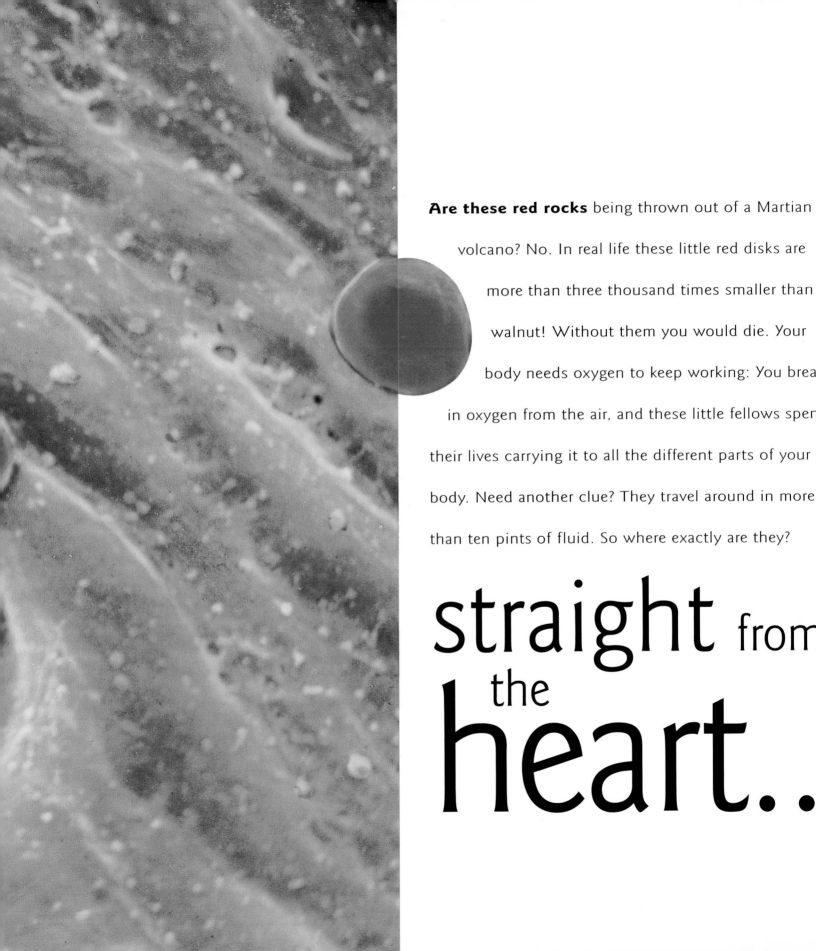

Are these red rocks being thrown out of a Martian volcano? No. In real life these little red disks are more than three thousand times smaller than a walnut! Without them you would die. Your body needs oxygen to keep working: You breathe in oxygen from the air, and these little fellows spend their lives carrying it to all the different parts of your body. Need another clue? They travel around in more than ten pints of fluid. So where exactly are they?

straight from the heart...

... this is *too* horrible

Imagine scuba diving across a coral reef. You're at peace in a silent, colorful world. Suddenly a violent wave throws you around. Acid eats away at you. Other chemicals begin to turn you to slush. You're being dragged down deeper and deeper into a black hole. Do you have the guts to survive? Or is something going to eat you for breakfast?

something to digest...

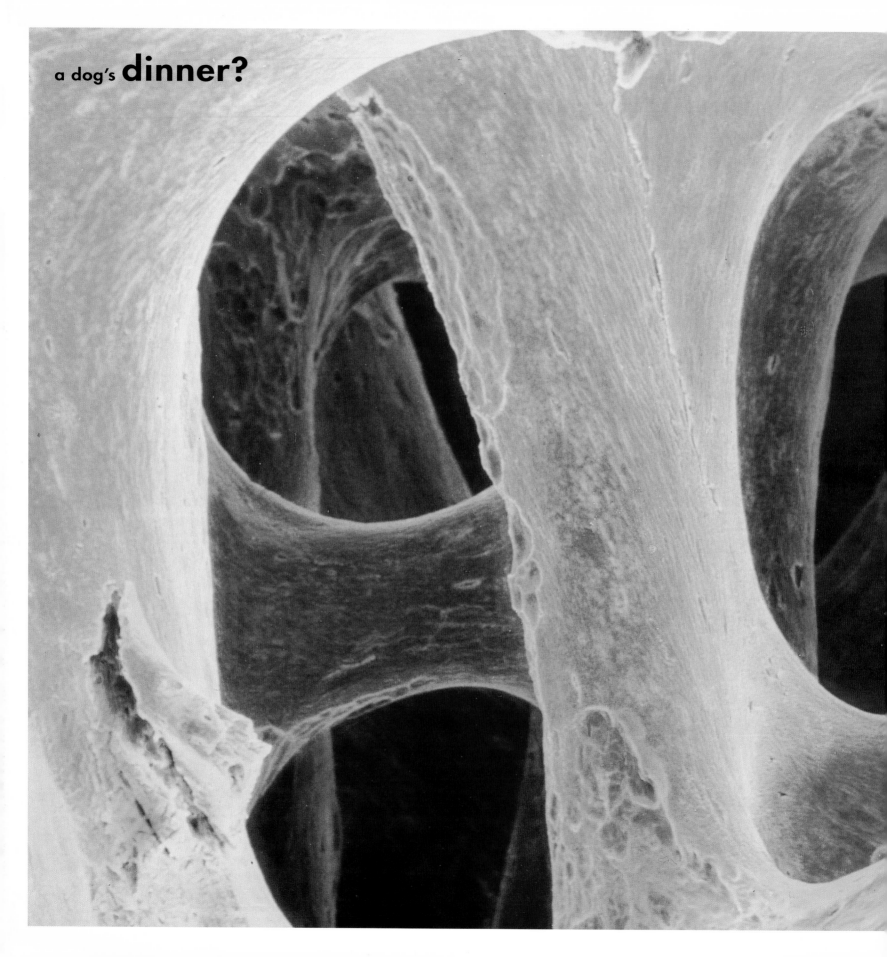

a dog's **dinner?**

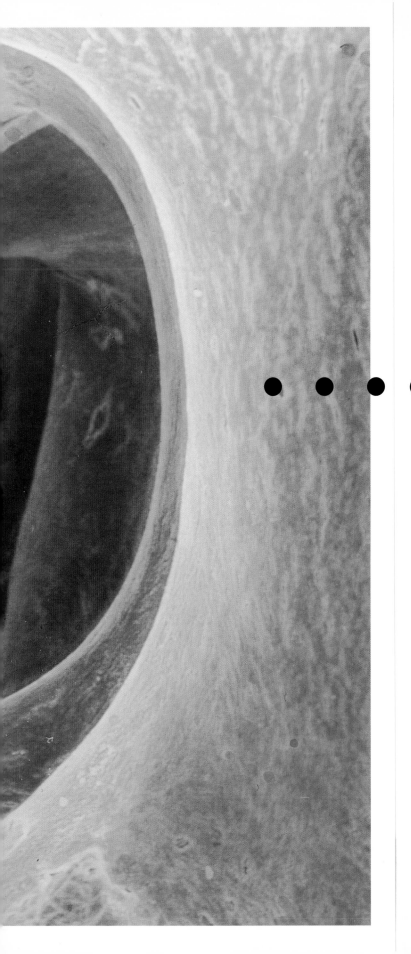

take a
.....break

Is it a spooky bat cave?

A forest at night? A honeycomb candy

bar? Well, you wouldn't want to eat it—unless

you were a dog—but it is handy stuff. Without it

you'd be just a quivering mass of jelly—no more than

a blob on the floor. Counting from your head to your

toes, you will find 206 of these in all different shapes and

sizes. They're tough, they're light, they're...

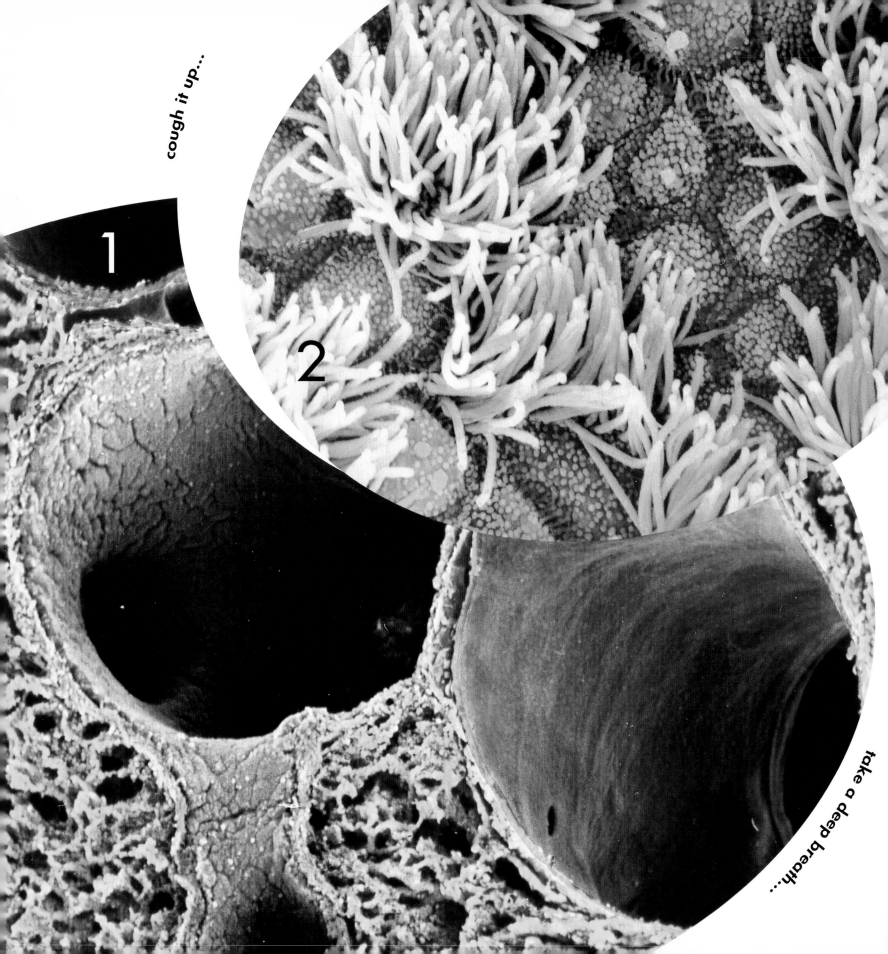

cough it up...

1

2

take a deep breath...

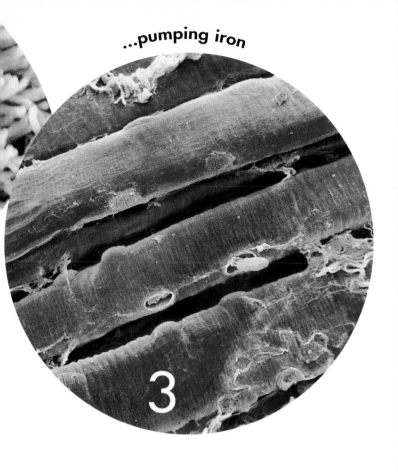

...pumping iron

3

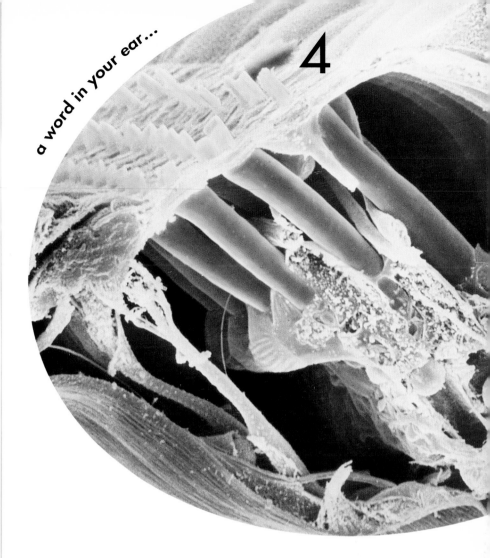

a word in your ear...

4

the Wacky world of...

Who needs outer space when you've got your own inner space! Imagine you've slimmed down to the size of a blood cell and then join us on an adventure into the deepest, darkest depths of your weird and wild interior. Have your tickets and cameras ready, please!

5

in the right vein...

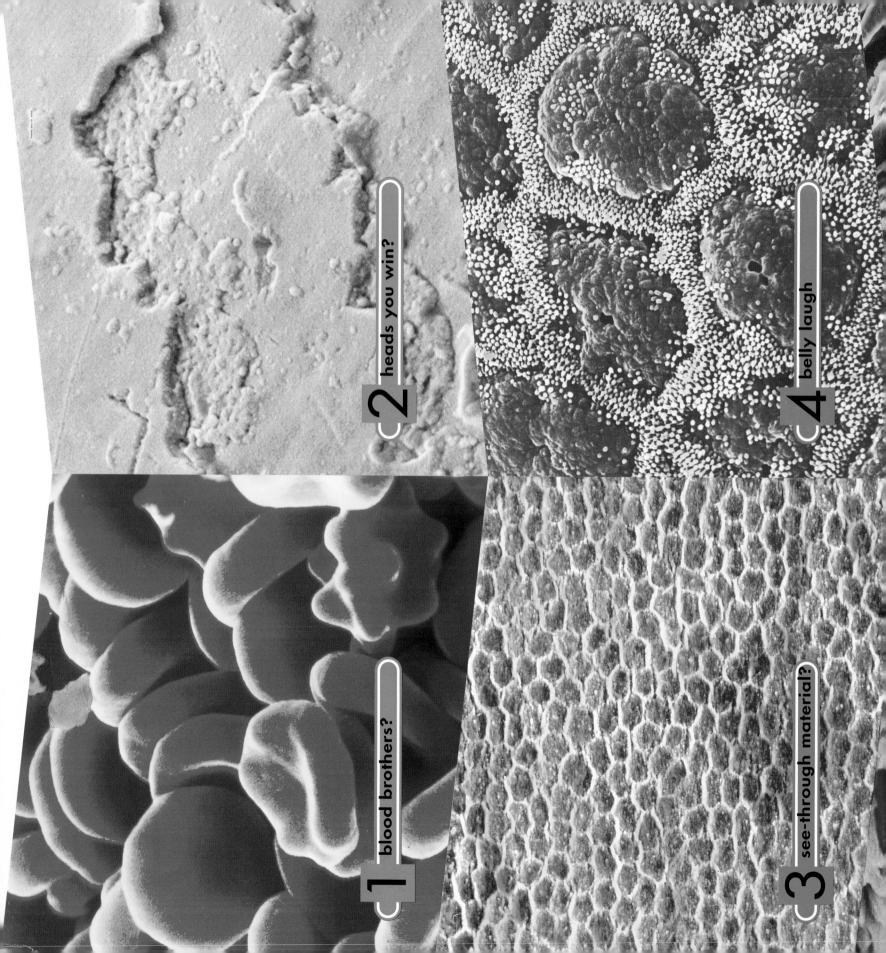

2 heads you win?

4 belly laugh

1 blood brothers?

3 see-through material?

6 tasty picture?

5 hard as...

quiztime...quiztime...quiztime...quiztime...quiztime...quiztime...quiztime...quiztime...quiztime...quiztime

...hasta la vista!